REEF ELEMENTARY SCHOOL

Hal S. Hammerhead

Frank Swordfish

Gary Barracuda

Jackie Puffer

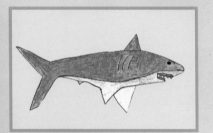

Butch G. White

Max H. S. Crab

Octo Octopus

Slick Tiger

Marvin G. W. Shark

Thomas B. Dolphin

Ty Sergeant

Stella B. Butterflyfish

Ruth S. Boxfish

Andy Triggerfish

For my brothers, Thomas and Jack

The fish and sea creatures in this book are common to the Hawaiian and Indo-Pacific waters. It is important to protect the reefs and ocean ecosystems so these beautiful animals can survive. A part of the proceeds from sales of this book will support marine conservation efforts. To learn more about these fish, check out the Fish Facts pages at the end of this book. To learn about about bullying and how to stop it, visit www.stopbullying.gov.

Special thanks to Keoki and Yuko Stender for providing fact-checking and most of the Fish Facts photographs. Visit www.marinelifephotography.com for more information about their work.

Reefs, sharks, and dolphin photographs from iStockphoto®

Marvin The Shark
Ages 3-10
Written and illustrated by Christopher John

 **Printed in the USA**

ISBN 978-0-9827951-4-9
Library of Congress Control Number: 2012938290

MARVIN
The Shark

Written and Illustrated by Christopher John

Once there was a shark named Marvin. He was a happy shark.

Marvin had more friends than you can imagine. Everyone treated him nicely.

One day, Marvin found out he had to move. There was just too much pollution in the water where he lived.

Marvin was going to move to Hawaii, where the water is warm and clean. The Hawaiian reefs are famous for beautiful coral and tons of fish.

His friends were sad and he was sad, too!

When Marvin arrived at his new school, he was a bit nervous about making friends.

During recess, Marvin went to the playreef. There he saw three sharks staring at him.

He noticed the other fish had scattered, which gave Marvin a bad feeling the rest of the day.

When Marvin was swimming home after school, he was stopped dead in his tracks by the same three sharks. He was surrounded with no one else in sight.

They teased Marvin because he was small for a great white.

The Shark Bullies kept nudging him and wanting to fight. But Marvin was a peaceful shark.

Finally, they got bored because Marvin wouldn't fight back, so they swam away.

Marvin swam home feeling blue.

The sad look on his face said it all. This place wasn't like his old reef.

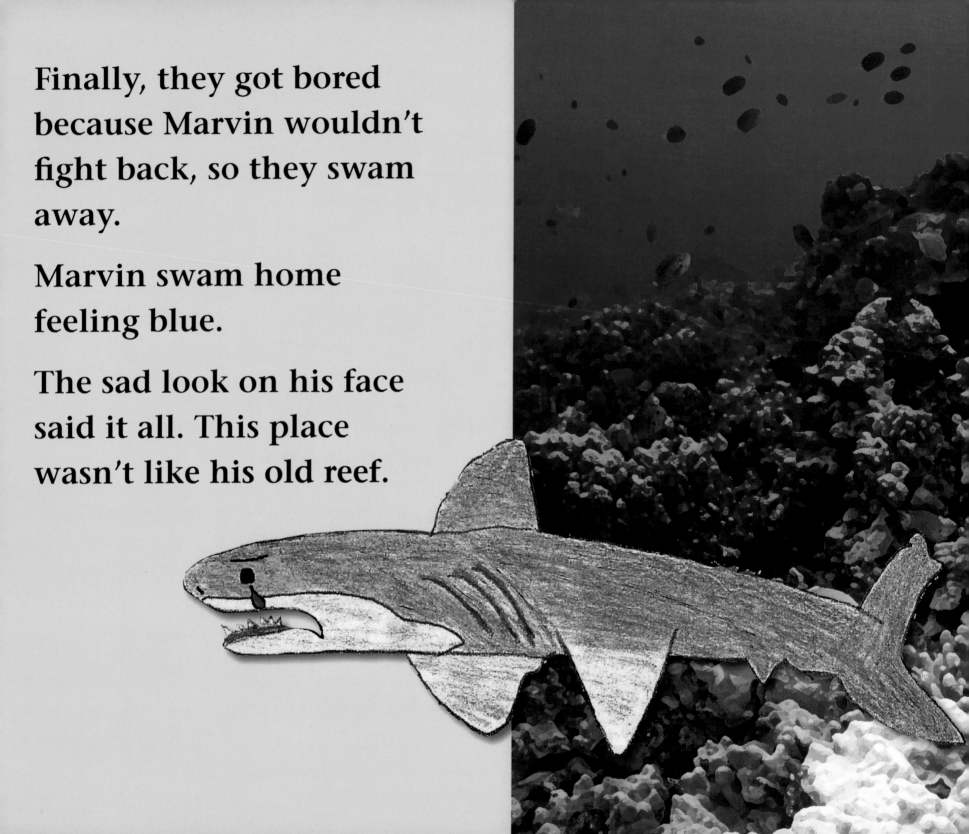

When Marvin was swimming to school the next day, he saw a big octopus talking to the Shark Bullies. He swam closer to hear what the octopus was saying.

Marvin heard the octopus teasing the sharks just like they had teased him!

Marvin knew he had to
help the three sharks.

In a splash, he swam in
to stop the octopus
from teasing them.

The octopus was
taken by surprise!
Marvin was so
brave for such
a little shark.

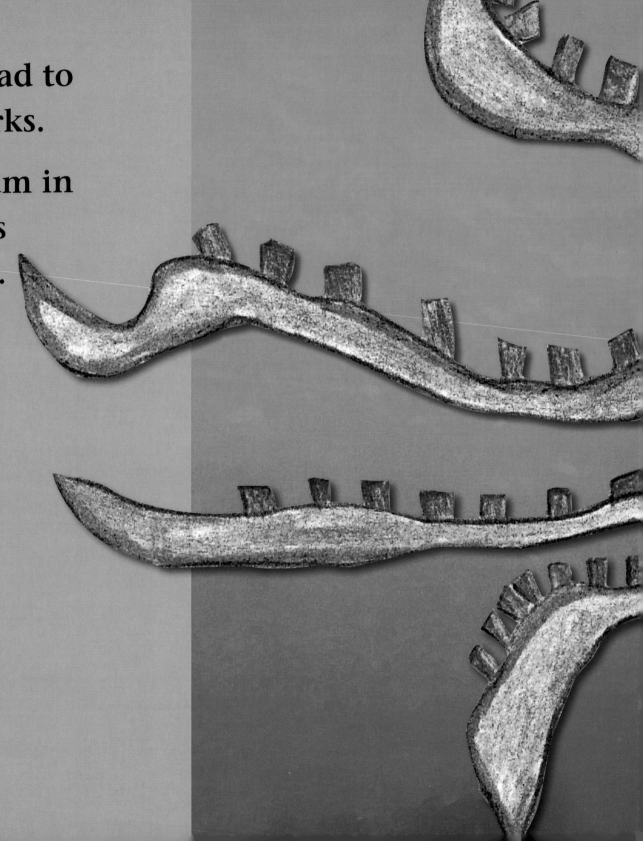

Octo's face suddenly changed. He was sorry for how he had treated the sharks. The other sharks saw what Marvin did and they felt sorry, too.

Just then Marvin had a thought. Maybe other fish are afraid of Octo because he is so big. It must be hard for him to make friends.

Poor Octo!

From that day on, they were all good friends. All of the sharks and Octo were nice and treated Marvin how he wanted to be treated.

Now, everyone got along —except for the new crab, Max. He didn't seem too happy to be there.

But that was a worry for another day.

Fish Facts

Tiger Shark

Galeocerdo cuvier

Size: 16–24 feet long; 1,200 lbs
Habitat: open waters of warm and temperate seas; shallow waters at night
Food: crustaceans, fish, seals, birds, squid, sea turtles, sea snakes

Tiger sharks are a near-threatened species. They have dark, wavy stripes that resemble a tiger's pattern. They hunt mainly at night.

Scalloped Hammerhead Shark

Sphyrna lewini

Size: 7–14 feet long; 300 lbs
Food: buried fishes and invertebrates
Habitat: tropical waters; 82 feet deep near shore; 1,600 feet deep in open water

Hammerheads are an endangered species. Their hammer-shaped head has eyes and nostrils at the tip. The design of their head allows them to sense prey buried under the sand as they sweep back and forth along the bottom. They often travel in schools.

Great White Shark

Carcharodon carcharias

Size: 20 feet long; 5,000 lbs
Food: fish, rays, smaller sharks, marine mammals
Habitat: temperate waters worldwide

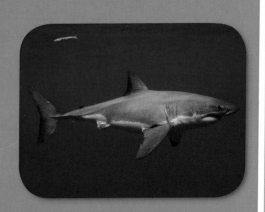

Great white sharks are highly endangered. Young sharks eat small fish, but large adults will hunt marine mammals and scavenge for dead carcasses. They do not consider humans prey, so most attacks are cases of mistaken identity. Great whites have rows of serrated teeth that are continually replaced. When a shark bites, it shakes its head from side to side. In one year, a great white can consume 11 tons of food. Great whites can live about 25 years.

Bottlenose Dolphin

Tursiops truncatus

Size: 8–13 feet long; 300–1,400 lbs
Food: small fish, crustaceans, squid
Habitat: tropical and temperate coastal waters of Pacific and Atlantic Oceans

Bottlenose dolphins are dark gray on the dorsal (top) side and lighter gray on the underside. This coloration helps camouflage them when swimming. They have a long snout with sharp teeth. Since they are mammals rather than fish, they breathe air through a blowhole on top of their head. Dolphins travel in groups called pods.

Bluestripe Butterflyfish

Chaetodon fremblii

Size: 5 inches maximum length
Habitat: tropical coral reefs from surface to 200 feet
Food: coral, small crustaceans, fish eggs, algae, zooplankton

If you ever go snorkeling or diving, you will likely see butterflyfish. They are found in abundance on healthy coral reef ecosystems around the world. The Bluestripe is one of 25 species of butterflyfish in Hawaii.

Indo-Pacific Sergeant

Abudefduf vaigiensis

Size: 7 inches maximum length
Habitat: tropical shallow reefs exposed to currents; shore outcroppings and ledges
Food: zooplankton

There are many species of sergeant, which are part of the damselfish family. They are found in warm seas around the world. The Indo-Pacific sergeant is one of two species common in Hawaii. The males are responsible for guarding the eggs. They actually change to a darker color when they are doing this job.

Spotted Boxfish

Ostracion meleagris

Size: 6 inches maximum length
Habitat: tropical coral reefs at any depth
Food: sponges, tunicates, hydroids, algae

Boxfish are named for their unusual structure—a body made of fused scales that form a boxlike shape. Eyes, mouth, gills, anus, and fins are openings in the box. All boxfish are born as dull-colored females. Only some grow up to become the vibrantly colored males.

Great Barracuda

Sphyraena barracuda

Size: 4 ½ –6 ½ feet long
Habitat: subtropical reefs; open waters up to 100 feet deep
Food: fish, squid, octopus, shrimp

Barracudas are powerful predators, hunting their prey using a wait-and-ambush technique. They can swim in short bursts up to 27 miles per hour. Their sharp, jagged teeth make them a fish to be wary of when swimming on the Hawaiian reefs. They are safe to watch as long as you don't wear shiny jewelry. Barracudas may mistakenly strike if the jewelry appears to look like shiny, small fish.

Lagoon Triggerfish

Rhinecanthus aculeatus

Size: 12 inches maximum length

Habitat: tropical reefs and sandy areas around them in waters up to 50 feet deep

Food: invertebrates, algae

Triggerfish are tough little fish with bodies perfect for protecting their nests against predators. Their scales are very hard and shaped like diamonds to form armor-like skin. They also have pointy spines. Triggerfish use their sharp teeth to break open shellfish, a favorite food.

Ornate Octopus

Callistoctopus ornatus

Size: arms up to 3 feet long; 10 lbs

Habitat: Pacific and Hawaiian reef flats and deeper waters

Food: crabs, lobster, snails, fish

Octopuses are not fish. They are cephalopods. Octopuses have four pairs of arms, two eyes, and a sharp beak. To protect themselves, they squirt ink or use camouflage. Some even change colors like a chameleon. Ornate octopuses are nocturnal, so you'll only see them at night. Most octopuses only live for about a year.

Stripebelly Puffer

Arothron hispidus

Size: 19 inches maximum length

Habitat: tropical rocky and sandy areas

Food: buried shellfish

Puffers have very loose skin, and they have no scales or pelvic fins. Puffers can "puff" up with water, which makes it hard for predators to eat them. Their spiny bodies are poisonous, so don't touch!

Hawaiian Swimming Crab

Charybdis hawaiensis

Size: 3 inches maximum width

Habitat: Hawaiian reefs and waters up to 60 feet deep

Food: algae, worms, small crustaceans, detritus (dead matter)

Swimming crabs are crustaceans, not fish. They have a pair of flattened legs shaped like paddles that are used for swimming. Being mainly nocturnal, they hide in crevices and antler coral during the day.